Run • Jump • Whiz • Splash

VERA ROSENBERRY

Run Jump

Whiz

Splash

HOLIDAY HOUSE / NEW YORK

Copyright © 1999 by Vera Rosenberry
All Rights Reserved
Printed in the United States of America
Book design by Vera Rosenberry & Sylvia Frezzolini Severance
First Edition

Library of Congress Cataloging-in-Publication Data
Rosenberry, Vera.
        Run, jump, whiz, splash / by Vera Rosenberry.—1st ed.
                p. cm.
        Summary: Illustrations and simple text describe some
sights and sounds associated with each season.
        ISBN 0-8234-1378-0
        [1. Seasons—Fiction.] I. Title.
PZ7.R719155Ru   1999
[E]—dc21   98-14060
                            CIP
                            AC

For Tanya and Raman

Summer
is when

the milky white moon rises up

And you

Run

barefoot
over cool, dewy grass

Catching lightning bugs in a jar.

Then you let them go.

Autumn
is when

the fluttery pile of dry leaves grows

And you  jump

so high
in the crunch and smell

And sink, sink, sink down,

the sky above.

Then you jump again.

Winter
   is when

the mill pond is snowy
and still

And you

on skates

across smooth, silver ice

As swans fly up
from pale dry reeds

And an old goose scolds.

Spring
    is when

the rain-filled creek bubbles and laughs

And you

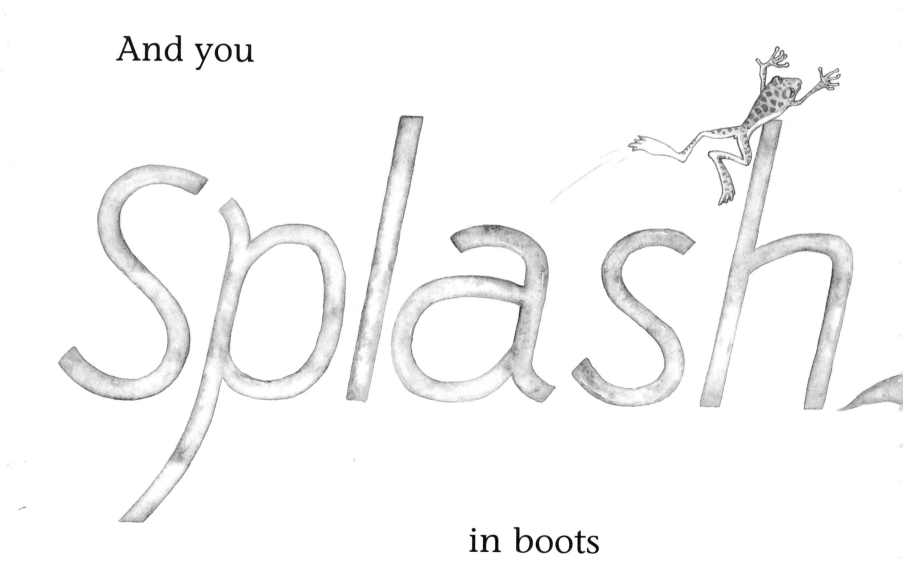

Splash

in boots

upstream through dripping woods

While bluebells nod
   in a clean, wet breeze

And green-tipped trees sway.

Run

Jump

Whiz

Splash

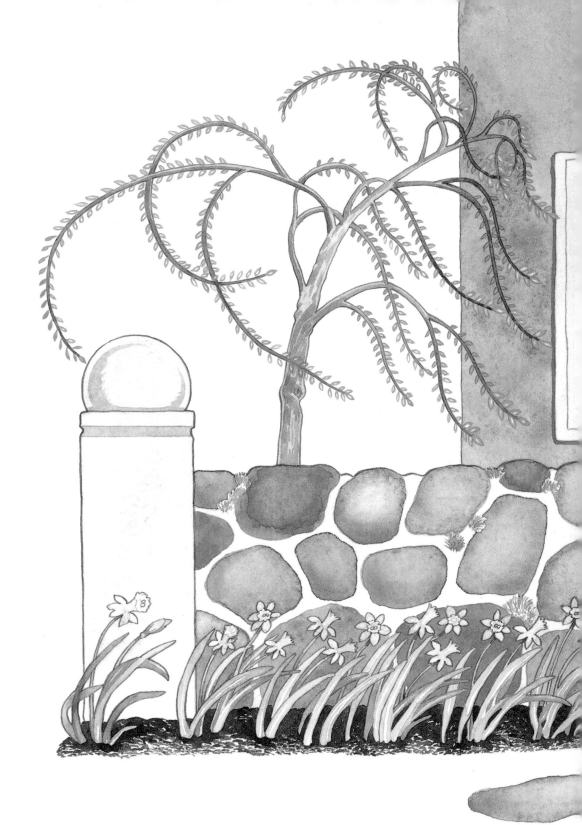

all the way home.